Juvenile

Ted E. Bear
Finds
Christmas

By Diane Mayfield

Illustrated by Miguel Diaz

IDEALS CHILDREN'S BOOKS

Copyright © MCMLXXXVIII by Hi-Mark International Teleproductions Corporation.
All rights reserved.
Printed and bound in the United States of America.
Published by Ideals Publishing Corporation
Nelson Place at Elm Hill Pike
Nashville, Tennessee 37214
ISBN 0-8249-8251-7

This is the story of how Ted Edward Bear found Christmas.

You see, bears sleep through Christmas— from about a quarter till winter to about half past spring. Most of them have never even heard of Christmas.

WELCOME TO BEARBANK

One year Ted decided to stay awake and look for Christmas. All the other bears laughed and made fun of him, but Ted didn't mind. He left Bearbank for the big city, confident he would find Christmas there.

Ted did find Christmas, and he was so excited that he wanted to tell his friends.

Once Ted was back home in Bearbank, he wanted to share his secret. He knew the other bears would see the big smile on his face and the twinkle in his eye. They would wonder what had happened to him. He was going to convince those bears that Christmas was real.

With confidence Ted said, "I'll show them that Christmas is much more than a story made up by humans. Why, it's . . . " Ted thought to himself for a moment. "Oh, where will I begin?"

Ted exclaimed, "I know, I'll find Patti and Professor Von Bear! They'll listen to me!"

He ran immediately to Bearwitness News, where he knew he would find these two friends still awake.

"Patti! Professor Von Bear!"

Patti Bear was happy to see Ted.

"Welcome home, Ted," she cried. "We missed you. Did you find Christmas?"

"Yah," said Professor Von Bear, "I want to hear any new factual data you discovered about this thing called 'Christmas'."

"I have so much to tell you," Ted began. "I've never seen anything as busy as Christmas."

"Even busier than downtown Bearbank during rush hour?" asked Patti.

"Yes," Ted answered. "People were hurrying home
carrying packages. Families were celebrating together.
There was a wonderful feeling in the air."

"Everyone was smiling and greeting each other, and there was such happiness. The people seemed to be singing:

Christmas, Christmas, we're glad
That Christmas is here."

"Big snowflakes were falling, carolers were singing, there was good cheer everywhere. Yes, it is true— Christmas is the happiest time of the year!"

"Then, over the happy, noisy sounds of the street, I heard some music. It was soft, gentle singing:
        Silent night, holy night . . ."

Patti asked, "Where did the music come from?"

"It came from inside a church," Ted said. "I went in to hear more and there I saw candles burning, and the light from them reflected off of beautiful stained glass windows.

"A choir continued to sing:
        Heavenly hosts sing alleluia.
        Christ the savior is born . . .

"There was a special light on the faces of those humans as they sang. Inside that church I found faith, hope, and love."

"The music of Christmas made my heart happy," Ted
continued. "And then I was too excited to even think about
going to sleep."

"But, Ted, did you find Christmas in the church?" asked Patti.

Ted answered thoughtfully, "Yes, I found part of it there."

"Then, as I walked through the big church doors to the street, I saw children crowding around a store window. Inside that window were some toys—toy soldiers, baby dolls, ballerinas, and clowns. They seemed to be saying 'Merry Christmas' to the boys and girls."

"The toy soldiers marched back and forth, saying,
　　It's a very merry, holly berry,
　　Happy Christmas day,
　　And we wish you all a Merry Christmas
　　In a Christmas way.
"Pretty ballerinas danced as they sang,
　　We're so glad that it is Christmas.
　　May the season bring you joy.
　　Merry Christmas! Merry Christmas!
　　Merry Christmas, girls and boys!
"Sweet baby dolls giggled and cooed their holiday

greeting:

> It's a very merry Christmas,
> And we wish you Christmas cheer,
> And we hope you keep this happy
> Christmas feeling through the year.

"And silly clowns turned somersaults as they began to shout,

> Merry Christmas! Merry Christmas!
> May the dreams you dream come true.
> Have a very merry Christmas,
> Merry Christmas to you!"

Ted continued his story. "I kept on looking for Christmas. I walked the streets, I looked inside the stores. I felt I was getting closer, and then I saw a big person with a white beard and a red suit. Children were lined up to talk with him. He seemed to be in charge of Christmas."

"It was Santa Claus!!" exclaimed Ted.

"You actually found Santa Claus?" asked Professor Von Bear. "Is it true, Ted, that he actually uses that primitive means of propulsion to fly around the world—a sleigh pulled by reindeer?"

"That's right, Professor Von Bear," Ted said.

"Ah hah!" shouted the professor. "Just wait until the other professors hear this! Now they will have to rewrite all of the physics books at Grizzly University!"

Ted insisted that it was true. And he added, "When I looked into Santa's eyes, I knew he could tell me where to find Christmas."

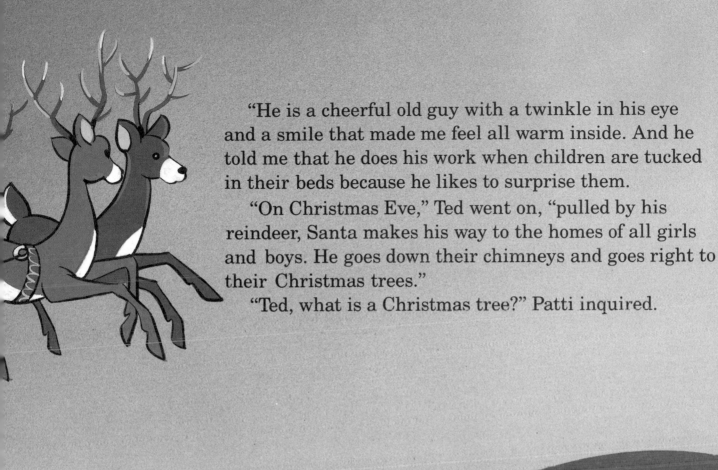

"He is a cheerful old guy with a twinkle in his eye and a smile that made me feel all warm inside. And he told me that he does his work when children are tucked in their beds because he likes to surprise them.

"On Christmas Eve," Ted went on, "pulled by his reindeer, Santa makes his way to the homes of all girls and boys. He goes down their chimneys and goes right to their Christmas trees."

"Ted, what is a Christmas tree?" Patti inquired.

Ted remembered well the beautiful trees he had so recently admired. How magical they had seemed! "A Christmas tree," he said, "is a big part of Christmas."

Professor Von Bear was taking notes as fast as he could, but he stopped to ask Ted, "If you have a big tree, do you have more Christmases?"

"No," Ted answered. "The size doesn't matter. It is what the tree stands for that makes it so special. Families everywhere each have their own tree, and they decorate it just as they see Christmas."

"A Christmas tree may be short or tall, fancy or plain. It
might not look perfect, but it always stands proud—and it
has a merry Christmas glow. You see, a Christmas tree is
really a symbol of boundless Christmas joy."

"And under the Christmas tree there are gifts. There may be only a few, or there may be a lot; but no matter how many there are, they are put there with love. All are filled with surprises for family and friends. They are wrapped in colorful ribbons and bows. And when they are opened, you hear 'ooos' and 'aaaahs' and 'thank yous.'

"These gifts under the Christmas tree bring happiness—not only because of what is inside them, but also because they are expressions of love."

Ted E. Bear's friends were beginning to like the idea of Christmas.

Patti said, "Oh, Ted, I think I understand what Christmas is. It is beautiful music and Christmas trees and packages waiting to be opened. But it is more than that. It's a way for people to get together—family, friends, and even people you pass on the street—a way of giving and of sharing love."

"That's right, Patti," said Ted. "And I learned that the best gifts we can give are those from our hearts, like love and peace and goodwill to all people—to *bears*, too! Yes, that's what Christmas is."

That evening, as Ted sat in his favorite chair, he began to feel drowsy. He stretched his arms and settled back. Outside, the winter snow was beginning to melt. Spring would soon be here. Then his friends would wake up and return from their winter hibernation vacations. Ted began to doze, and as he slept, his dreams were all about Christmas.